CW01500458

The Tudor Mystery

Authors Note

What follows serves as an introduction to the full series of books in the Tudor Mystery Trials. In the first novel in the series, A Queen's Spy, we meet Richard Fitzwarren again five years after the events which unfold here.

†

Historical Background

In the summer of 1548 Princess Elizabeth, daughter of Henry VIII, lived with her stepmother, Katherine Parr. Katherine was Henry's last wife and survived him when he died in 1547. Before becoming Queen of England, Katherine Parr had been betrothed to the dashing Admiral Sir Thomas Seymour, and after Henry's death Katherine turned to her first love and they married within months of her becoming a widow.]

Elizabeth and Katherine had become close during the final years of Henry's reign and it seemed only natural that the Princess should remain under her governance, so she became a part of the Seymour household. In 1548 a scandal reached even the ears of the Privy Council; something had happened at Seymour's house. There was even a rumour that the Lady Elizabeth was with child. These are facts; the rest is fiction.

July 1548

They found them together in the garden. Alone!

Elizabeth was crying, cheeks red and puffy. She had been sobbing for some time. On her arm a set of bruises; the tell-tale shadow left where a hand had gripped it hard, and a grazed shoulder told where the cloth from the dress had scored her skin as it had resisted before finally ripping. Her bodice was rent apart and shaking hands clutched desperately at the material trying to pull the torn edges together. Fiery auburn curls spilt from the neat pile beneath a cap and lay on shaking shoulders in uneven curled locks.

They could only guess what he had done to her - and guess they did. The Lady had obviously tried to defend herself and his shirt was ripped down the front, and across his cheek he wore an ugly set of lines, ripped by her nails as he set upon her. He was breathing deeply from the attack and they knew they had arrived just in time to save her honour. The Master had sent them to look for the Lady, telling them she was in danger, and he had been right.

There were no questions asked. He was overpowered easily by the four them and indeed he didn't fight as they disarmed him and led him from the garden pinioned between the largest two of them. Someone had sent one of the Lady's servants and she was quickly led from the scene of the attack wrapped in a borrowed cloak, hastened indoors away from prying eyes, still sobbing and her governesses supporting arm tight around her shoulders.

✝

Kate, Elizabeth's governess - close to tears herself - tried again, "Please, we have to know what happened?"

Still, Elizabeth would not reply and Kate couldn't make her speak, however much she wanted to shake some sense into her. The girl sat, her tear streaked face frozen, and refused to speak, her eyes fastened on the floor.

Kate hardened her tone, "Elizabeth you must tell us. I can see what he has done to your dress, what else did he do?"

Still nothing.

"Did he try to kiss you? Did he lay his hands upon you? I know these are terrible questions my sweet, but I have to know. *They* have to know." Kate pleaded, squeezing both of Elizabeth's shoulders gently.

Elizabeth just shook her hands off and continued to stare fixedly at the floor.

"I'll have to go and see them, Elizabeth; we'll talk when I get back. I'll leave you with Anne," Kate said, then added as Elizabeth looked up mournfully, "I will not be long."

Kate left the room and went along the corridor. The door to the solar was closed and she could hear heated voices inside. Under the circumstances, she was not surprised. Knocking gently, she waited to be admitted.

When she was bid enter, she found Thomas Seymour stood near the window, his back to his wife, Katherine Parr. Elizabeth's stepmother was clearly in a state of distress.

Seymour turned, "What's he done to her then?" he snarled, "I'll cut off more than his bloody ears for this."

Kate bobbed a curtsey, "She'll not say, my lord. I'm sure I will have the truth soon, but I think Lady Elizabeth is still too shocked over what has happened."

"I'm not bloody surprised," Thomas Seymour continued, "I blame myself. To think that it was because of me that she came into contact with that churl."

"Sir, its not your fault; we all should have seen it. He spent too much time with Elizabeth and he's older than her." A tear came to Kate's eyes, "I just thought she was walking in the garden. If I'd known he was there I would not have let her go alone, I'm so sorry."

"Sit, Kate, please," Katherine said from behind a wet silken handkerchief, "we are all sorry, and it was not your fault." Then looking over at Seymour she added, "Was it, Thomas?"

Seymour turned back to gaze from the window, "No, not at all." Then, gathering his thoughts, he suddenly seemed to feel the need to absent himself from his wife's company. "I need to deal with this, please excuse me," and with the hastiest of bows to his wife, he left.

Katherine waited until the door closed before turning her gaze on Kate. "How is Elizabeth?"

"I don't know M'Lady, she won't speak, but who can blame her. She's only just fourteen, she didn't deserve such treatment at the hands of a man," Kate said, and more tears loosed themselves down her cheeks. "They should cut his hands off; indeed give me the axe and I would do it myself."

Katherine didn't comment, instead she said, "go, be with Elizabeth, she needs you. Please tell me how she fares."

Kate, wiping her face clean and straightening her skirts, assumed once again her air of calm and returned to Elizabeth's room. There she found the girl out of her ripped dress and in bed. The curtains had been drawn against the summer light and the room was hot and stuffy with more than a few insects trapped, their escape to the garden now cut off by the closed windows.

"Anne, get rid of that, burn it! We never want to see it again," Kate said indicating the ripped dress that hung over the chair back.

The sight of the torn threads pulled from their weft in the fabric brought tears back to her eyes. The dress was one Kate herself had helped Elizabeth embellish by stitching tiny seed pearls along the sleeve edges to make small pristine white flowers. All that time. All wasted. The tears fell down her face. Damn him to Hell.

†

They'd locked him in a storeroom, which was the most secure place they could find at Seymour's house, and placed a guard on the door.

"Let me in," ordered Seymour. His men obliged and unlocked the door.

The door closed behind him and the other man stood; they looked at each other coldly.

"Well," said Seymour, "wrong place at the wrong time. What a pity, we were getting along so well."

"I would say right place at the right time," Richard replied from where he leant against the barrels in the store room.

"No, I think you'll soon be agreeing with me," Seymour said. "You'll stop in here for a few days, time enough for a letter to reach your father informing him of what has happened and then you can get yourself gone wherever you wish."

"And that's it?" Richard asked incredulously.

"That will indeed probably be it for you. I can't see you surviving this scandal, can you?" said Seymour.

"But I didn't do anything!" blurted Richard.

"You'll be the only one who'll ever believe that," Seymour said, and turned, closing the door behind him.

Richard stared at the door, his anger barely contained, frustrated beyond endurance for there was nothing he could do, and he knew it. Richard pressed his hands to his eyes; he knew Seymour only too well and he knew he rarely made idle threats. Every move he made was one to take him closer to the throne, to the seat of power, and he protected his position like an errant knight on the chess board. His pawns were information, and he held so much on so many that there were few felt any desire to cross Thomas Seymour. Richard had worked in some small capacity for him as scribe and messenger and he knew some of those that Seymour kept in his employ. Seymour played for power, and he knew the power of secrets only too well.

✝

Halfway through the journey from the store room back to see his wife, Seymour had pressed his mind to the problem and found a solution. By the time he laid his hand on the door to where his wife waited he had a smile on his face and a course of action to follow that would indeed lead to an advantage. Katherine, pregnant with their first child, would be the easiest part.

Thomas paused outside the door, observed a sleeve, the velvet slashed to reveal the cream shirt beneath. The trials of the day had twisted the shirt beneath and no longer did the symmetric puffs of white show neatly through the doublet. Seymour took a few moments to pinch the linen back to perfection before he applied his hand to the door.

"My love," he opened the door and knelt at the side of her seat, taking her hand, "what a terrible strain on you, I am so sorry. He has, of course, confessed."

"Confessed," Katherine said a little shocked.

"Indeed," Seymour confirmed, there was, of course, no confession, but that would be a formality only.

Katherine looked incredulous; she had caught Elizabeth on her husband's knee a week ago! The girl had fled and he had explained it away as nothing other than a silly game a parent would play with a child. Katherine remained uneasy, she had seen the look on her husband's face that day before he saw her and she was sure he had been kissing Elizabeth.

"I blame myself, I really do. He's not suitable company for Elizabeth, I should have seen it, and I worry that it has upset you, my love," Thomas raised his wife's hand, turned it over and kissed her palm, holding her eyes with his as he did. "It was good that they caught him when they did, that poor girl, and my poor Lady."

Katherine smiled, "you are ever my gallant Thomas."

"I waited a long time, my Lady, for you," Thomas smiled and raising her chin with his hand, he kissed her slowly, "I vowed to keep you happy and I stand by that my love; always."

Katherine ran her hand down his cheek, "Ah my love,"

"So I will write to his father first and then decide what is best to do with him," Thomas said, "he is no concern of yours. I will ensure that everything is as it should be. Worry not my love,"

Katherine, needing to be reassured, soaked up his words and pushed the doubt to the back of her mind. *A pregnant fantasy, many women have them, she told herself.*

✝

Kate gave up in the end. Elizabeth would stubbornly say nothing about what had happened in the garden. Thomas Seymour had sent for her again and questioned her at length, but there was little she could tell him. Eventually he had seemed satisfied and dismissed her. If Kate thought that was the end of the matter though, she was very wrong. Three days later she was summoned again into Thomas Seymour's presence and this time he was not alone. Beside him were Sir William Herbert and John Russell, both members of the Privy Council and friends of Thomas Seymour, and both were intent on finding out what exactly had happened in the garden.

She retold everything she knew, not that it was much. Then they pressed her with more questions about the Fitzwarren boy; was he oft in her company? Did he seek her out? How long had they had a friendship? Had she caught him before? Did she believe the Lady Elizabeth might be with child? When were her courses due? When had they last occurred? Kate's eyes were wide with fright. They truly believed her charge was with child, and by the end of the interview, Kate herself was also unsure.

Dismissed to an ante room to wait she sat wringing her hands. Why would the blasted girl say nothing? If she would say something it would only go towards her defence surely? The boy had confessed, so Lord Seymour had said, so what did she have to gain by her silence?

Eventually, she was summoned back to the room and a white sheet of paper placed before her.

"It's merely a record of what we have spoken about," Sir Thomas said, his manner offhand, "If you would be so kind as to sign after your name we will require you no more."

The scribe who had obviously prepared the document passed her a pen and pointed to where her name was and the vacant space left for her own signature.

Kate paused, unsure.

"You can write?" Seymour asked, his eyes rolling in his head. "Carter here will sign your name by proxy…"

"I can write Sir," Kate said gripping the pen with fury.

"Well then," he pressed.

"Should I not read it…?" She asked. It was a full sheet and would take more than a few minutes to read.

"It's just a record of what we talked about, woman. Now get it signed and be gone," Thomas growled. "These gentlemen here have little time to waste,"

Kate signed her full name, Katherine Ashley, where they indicated and lay the pen on the desk. As soon as she had finished, the sheet disappeared from in front of her into Seymour's keeping. Her eyes had little time to see what was written; starting at the top she had been able to read the preamble only. *On this day, I, Katherine Ashley, Governess and member of the household of our most gracious Lady Elizabeth Tudor, Daughter of Henry VIII and Anne Boleyn, and most...* She had not managed to read more than this.

"Go woman, see to your charge."

Kate bobbed a curtsey and made her way quickly from the room.

†

When they were all gone Thomas Seymour smiled. He had all of the pieces of the puzzle now completed and all the evidence he needed, should he ever be required to use it, was in his hands. He could prove that the Lady Elizabeth was no longer a virgin; he had Kate's corroboration and he had Richard Fitzwarren's confession. His father, William Fitzwarren, had agreed to the bargain and was more interested in a place on the Privy Council and all the benefits that would bring; if it cost him a son, then that was a small price indeed.

As it was, Richard was secured in the house for eight days while Seymour laid out all his plans and secured all the participants' cooperation. In the end, it was not Seymour who came to tell him he was free to go, but his steward. Richard had expected to see Seymour again but was told he was away and that Richard should also make himself absent from the house very quickly as his presence was no longer to be tolerated. His possessions had already been collected and put in a pack and his horse saddled. The steward escorted him silently to the stables and bid him get his backside off Sir Seymour's property. He had little choice but to return home and to explain what had happened. Surely his family would believe him when he told them he had arrived just in time to save the Lady's honour. His mind wandered again over those events, a few moments only that had led him to spend eight long days alone in the dark, dank room.

✝

He had heard them before he saw them. A man's voice, the words were indistinct but the tone was playful and then he started to laugh. Quickly there had followed the sound of material ripping, a harsh searing noise, and then her scream followed by a plea, "No, no."

Richard had rounded the corner of the garden hedge and found them then. Her dress was ripped from neck to waist and lay open; her hands were trying to push away Seymour who lay on top of her. He already had himself ready for the act he sought to perform and had only to rid her of the last of her clothes to complete it.

Seymour was no small man and Richard fastened his hands into the back of his jacket and tried to pull him off the struggling girl.

"God's bones!" Seymour had exclaimed as he felt himself being dragged from the woman beneath him. He let go of one of her wrists and the flailing hand caught Richard across the cheek, the nails biting deep into his skin.

"You'll regret this, boy," was all he had said. On his feet in a moment, he grabbed Richard by the front of his jacket and threw him backwards, tearing his shirt and sending him sprawling over a low box hedge. Then he left the pair of them, the girl half-naked on her back and Richard on his knees staring at him.

Richard looked away from Elizabeth, not knowing what to say.

That was how it had been, a few moments only. Then they had found them both and Richard had been thrown into the storeroom; surely his father would believe him? Surely!

†

Seymour clenched his right hand, held it tightly with his left and squeezed his eyes tight in thought. He was thirty-eight, so old already, and still, he had not what he wanted. The old King's death should have been the moment he was able to place a controlling hand on the affairs of England, and yet it was his brother, Edward, who had managed to secure his place as Edward's protector. William Paget, one of Henry's chief advisors had been a willing tool in his brother's hand. Thomas had no doubt at all that his brother had promised much to Paget to get Henry's will changed before it was finally stamped. There was not a chance that Henry would have left power in the hands of a council of sixteen so heavily weighted in his brother's favour.

Why could nobody else see it? Why did they not speak out against Edward? Why had they let themselves be bent to his will?

The will had excluded the hardened Catholic Bishop Gardiner from the council, and himself, and the balance then swayed in the Reformist direction. His brother played them like fools, they viewed Edward Somerset, Uncle of the new king, as the ideal man to help the reformed religion spread and to keep at bay the Catholic hounds.

The bloody fools.

Thomas cursed under his breath; he hated to dwell on the smooth and easy passage his brother had taken to become Lord Protector, Henry's bloody successor in all but name. The child was nine! Nine years old only. Edward could do what he liked for near enough the next decade, the power rested in his hands. Thomas felt the blood start to pound in his temples as it always did.

The next closest route to putting a softly-clad shoe on the step to the throne was to marry into the family; an outside bet but it had been one Thomas had pressed for. If he could marry Edwards's half-sister, Elizabeth, then he would not only be a part of the Tudor dynasty but should the sister ever grace the throne then certainly he would be the guiding hand. So far though nothing had gone to plan. The stupid girl had spurned his advances; indeed she had returned his initial letter asking for her hand in marriage along with a candid reply telling him she would be in mourning for two years for her father. Frustrated and hot-headed, Thomas had changed direction like a galleon in a gale and had taken up his courtship once again of Katherine Parr. Katherine and he had planned to wed until Henry's eye had settled on what would be his final wife and Thomas had found himself exiled, albeit nobly, as a foreign ambassador. Frustrated and humiliated, Seymour had been put out of harm's way whilst the King availed himself of the widowed Katherine. With Henry dead, Thomas could now marry the Lady, and the Lady was not only now wealthy but she was also stepmother to Princess Elizabeth.

Like a sheepdog, Thomas Seymour doggedly pursued his pieces even if he had little idea what to do with them when they were his. Married now to Katherine, Elizabeth was also part of his household, and Thomas began to pay court to her as well. If Henry could swap wives as often as he liked, Thomas didn't think it would be too hard to move from Katherine to Elizabeth when the time was right.

Now though, there was a problem. The idiot girl - who had welcomed his touches, his gifts and his company - had screamed for help when he'd thought to show her the extent of his love. He could not believe the amount of time he had wasted on the bitch, to have her slap him across the face when he'd come to her in love's desire only to show her how much he adored her. The solution to the problem had turned up and had been boxed in a store room, and would, he had no doubt, take the blame for the Lady's distress. If needed, he would take the blame for the loss of the Lady's virginity as well. That would serve the hell-cat right for spurning his advances.

†

Elizabeth saw him coming towards her, casting her eyes around her wildly she realised he had engineered it so that there was to be no help at hand; they were alone. Straightening her back, raising her chin imperiously she stared at him with cold green eyes.

Thomas smiled.

"Well Lady, the trouble you have put me to," he said, hitching himself up on the edge of a table.

"Trouble?" She retorted, her voice icy, "I think, Sir Thomas, trouble is what you have cause to deliver on to me."

Thomas laughed, "Keep your words, Lady, the facts are simple, and base enough for even you to understand. You were caught in the garden, my dear with Fitzwarren, and he has confessed that you are no longer a maiden."

Elizabeth's eyes widened. Wisely, she chose to say nothing.

"So, the choices are fairly clear. He will, I have no doubt, keep his mouth shut and if you do likewise then I shall keep his written confession to myself. Unless of course, you wish the world to know you are little better than your mother?"

Rising from the table, he walked the few steps towards her and put his hand under her chin; Elizabeth thought he was going to make to kiss her and recoiled.

"Think on it," Thomas said, and then added, "you and I would be better as friends. Am I not still your favourite Admiral?"

Elizabeth had been a victim of his easy charm, shining brightly in the light of his compliments and attention. In the world of the court, true friends were few and she had thought of him as one; maybe a little too close a friend but she had not seen the danger in the game she had played with a man nearly three times her age, having no idea where the laughter and closeness they shared would lead.

"I am sure we can still be friends," Elizabeth agreed, conceding nothing but wishing him gone and recognising that he wished to continue their now tarnished relationship as it had been before he set upon her in the garden.

August 1548

Stop!

"Pull that rope tighter," he heard his father's words, and the answering tug as the rope securing his arms around the tree was yanked tighter. His wrists nearly, but not quite, met on the other side of the trunk; his cheek was pressed to the bark and another rope around his waist to the tree meant he was completely immobile. That was how they wanted him.

"He'll not move now," he heard his brother's voice on the other side of the tree where he had just finished pulling the rope tight. He guessed right that his brother had twisted a wood stick into the rope to wind it taut. The pressure on his shoulders was almost unbearable as the rope sought to tear the joints apart. A coarse knot in the trunk bit painfully into his cheek and another was cutting through his shirt into his chest.

"Stop, please! What are you doing?" his words were indistinct as his face was pressed that hard to the tree.

"Shut up, I'll not listen to your lies." His father's voice came from behind him. "You've dragged my name into the gutter, you filthy, lecherous wretch. Seymour was a friend; how could you?"

"I didn't do anything," he tried but he knew they were not listening.

Richard couldn't see them but he could hear them behind him and also the noise from the unsettled horses tethered not far away. He tried to pull against the rope and found himself screaming as his right shoulder twisted painfully in the socket.

Then there was laughter.

"I haven't touched you yet," His father said, then to his brother, "Here, hold that"

There was silence and then some shuffling. Then he realised what they meant to do. He heard the whip as it cut its way through the air and then he felt it as it slit the linen shirt and carved a red track across his back.

The boy bit his lip so hard, blood welled from his mouth.

Four more followed in quick succession.

"Please," he begged, tears ran down his face to mix with the blood pouring from his mouth. His voice was quiet and he knew they did not hear him, and even if they could they did not care.

"Let me have a go!" said an eager voice.

Then his brother took up the whip and he put every ounce of his strength into the strokes he dealt, eager to impress his father. Their father.

Before his brother had finished the blackness had claimed him. His head hung limply. The ropes holding him in place cut brutally into his flesh as they bore his full weight now that his legs had buckled.

Steven watched. There were tears on his face and he had to look away as each new stroke was laid on the young mans back. From where he was concealed he could hear their laughter and he'd heard the boy's screams which, thankfully, had now stopped.

The shirt was shredded and his back was cut raw. Robert's strokes were not as accurate as his father's and Steven could see some of the lash strokes had laid across his shoulders. Blood dripped in a steady stream to the forest floor. *Please God, make them stop, please let them stop.* Had they not done enough? Steven closed his eyes to shut out the horror and prayed. Prayed to God to still William Fitzwarren's hand; prayed to God to save the boy; prayed for an end to the horror; prayed for the noise in his ears of the whip smacking into the maimed flesh to stop.

Make it stop, make it stop!

William Fitzwarren looked at the whip in his hand; even the leather-bound handle was now sticky with blood. He threw it on the ground. Picking up the doublet they had ripped from his son's back, he wiped his hands clean, then dropped it unheeding.

"Come on, it's getting dark," William said to his son.

Steven let out a shuddering breath; they had stopped. *Thank you, Lord, thank you.*

"What about his horse?" Robert Fitzwarren asked his father.

"You have it; he's not going to be needing it again is he?" William said.

"Really? Thank you father," Robert's face beamed and he untied the reins to Richard's horse. It was a far better horse than his own: his brother had lavished hours on training.

"Of course," William said, smiling benevolently at his son, "ride it back now, why not? See how he feels."

Robert quickly let the stirrups down; he was a hand taller than Richard. Satisfied, he mounted and patted the horse's neck.

Steven watched them, his prayers had resumed and now he asked God to remove them so he could see to the lad. The bloody body tied to the tree did not move and hung limply against the supporting bonds.

"I'll take your horse," William was saying, "You go ahead and get a feel for how he rides,"

Robert pressed his heels into the horse and set off and William, gathering the reins of the riderless horse, made to follow.

Steven waited until he was sure they were gone. He could no longer hear the sounds of the hooves and he knew they were probably in the meadow now, outside the forest and on their way back to the Manor.

Steven had little stomach for his task. He tried to keep his eyes from the scored flesh and the thick blood running in globules down the cuts. It was June and warm, and the flies were already starting to feast.

"Away with you," Steven waved the insects away; retrieving the jacket William had carelessly dropped, he laid it gently over Richard's destroyed back.

"Lad, can you hear me? Richard?" Steven lifted his head but the boy was unresponsive. Steven was even unsure as to whether or not he lived. If there was breath coming from his torn lips, he could not tell.

Taking his knife from his belt, he cut the bottom rope first and felt the body sag heavily on the top rope. The twists of cord around his wrists had cut cruelly into the flesh and his hands were purple. Steven held his arm as he cut the top rope but was unprepared for the weight of the boy as his body, released from its bonds, fell backwards onto the forest floor.

"Sorry lad, sorry," Steven bent over the crumpled form. There was no sign of life, his face beneath the filth and blood was deathly white and he could see no rise and fall of his chest. Steven pressed his knuckles into his eyes as the tears came.

There was a choking cough from the body on the floor.

Steven, his hand slippery in the spilt blood, rolled Richard on to his side, and he was sick onto the dusty forest floor.

"Lad, can you hear me? Master? It's me, Steven," he tried, holding him as more vomit poured from his mouth.

The boy's body shook; harsh gasps escaped him as the pain resonated through his body.

"I…hear," was all he managed.

"Good lad, I don't know how but I'll get you out of here. It's going to hurt, and I'm sorry, but I'm going to have to get you on to your feet," Steven said.

There was a noise which he took to be an acceptance of his help. Steven began then the slow process of getting him to his feet.

"Come on, I'll get you out of here."

✝

Steven looked at himself. He was covered in blood, none of it his own, and he had needed to strip his own shirt and jacket before he returned to Fitzwarren's house. Richard wanted some of his belongings and he'd made Steven promise to fetch them for him. Being the family priest he could come and go as he pleased, no-one would suspect him of anything. William had left his son for dead and would be waiting for someone to find him and report the incident, so time was on his side. No one noted his passing and he was able to collect the few possessions Richard had asked him to bring; a sword, a small amount of money and a leather bag that he had found exactly where Richard had told him it would be, secretly stowed in a recess at the back of the fireplace. It was little enough to start a new life with, but it would have to do.

September 1548

Elizabeth refused to speak further of the incident Kate never got a word from her on the matter. Shortly afterwards Elizabeth was sent away to live with Sir Anthony Denny and his wife, sister of Elizabeth's beloved governess Kate; and Katherine Parr went into confinement with her first child. At the age of thirty-seven it was never going to be an easy birth. She gave Thomas a daughter and begged him to send for her own surgeon to attend her, but Thomas delayed and Katherine weakened and died six days after bringing their daughter, Mary, into the world. Disillusioned at the end, she finally saw through her dashing husband's façade and realised she was about to allow him to take the next step in his twisted plan. Her death, she realised, would leave him free to court Elizabeth.

Indeed within weeks, Thomas had sent messages to find out about the extent of the Princess's wealth, which properties she owned, their state of repair and the amount of her personal finances. Katherine Parr, had sadly been right. Thomas immediately pressed for Elizabeth's hand, writing to her personally and also enquiring of her steward what properties she held and what her annual income was. Elizabeth had rebuffed him, telling him that she would be in mourning for her father for two years. His brother had been furious of Thomas' advances as had been the Privy Council. Despite his efforts, it was, for the moment, a dead end.

January 1549

Thomas turned his attentions instead to his nephew, Edward VI. Edward was ten years old and he liked Thomas. He was the uncle who treated him well, reminded him of his sovereignty, of his rights. If there was gift or a new amusement it was generally Thomas who would have brought it to the boy.

So greed had taken Thomas this further step. If his brother, Edward, could be the King's protector, then why could Thomas not have the role? Surely the boy preferred him, and if he decreed that Thomas become his protector then he would be unassailable. Royal power was royal power even if it was vested in such young hands.

✝

Edward broke off a small piece of marchpane, and waved it in front of the spaniel's nose.

"You want it Bragge? Well you will have to work for it," the boy said, snapping his fingers. His eyes widened with delight as the spaniel obediently sat back on its haunches and begged for the sweet meat.

"Look Uncle, I have trained him, see," Edward said. Then he threw the yellow treat the spaniel snapping it from the air and swallowing it instantly, its eyes now fixed on the plate still full of marchpane sitting on the table at his master's elbow.

"Very good, very good," Thomas said clapping his hands.

"He can do more, watch this," Edward said, delighted by his uncle's praise. He took two marchpane flowers and his small child's hands quickly squashed them and moulded them until there emerged from his sticky fingers a small mouse, complete with a short lumpy tail. "Now you will see how well I have trained him."

Edward put the mouse-like lump on the floor some way distant from Bragge, his eyes on the spaniel. "Bragge, watch," The spaniel lay down slowly, shoulders hunching, eyes fastened on the mouse.

"Uncle, Uncle, see him now!" Edward grasped the marchpane tail and swished the mouse from side to side. The dog's head snapped round to follow the handmade rodent, eyes fixed on the prey, ears cocked and the claws, almost cat like, gripped the carpet ready to pounce when the order came.

"Bragge is a loyal servant, Your Grace, all your subjects should obey you as well," Thomas said, smiling.

Edward picked up the mouse and dropped it only a hands span from the spaniel's paws. "See he will not take it until I issue the command."

The spaniel's attention was completely fastened on the mouse now; slaver had begun to pour from his mouth sullying the fine face and beautiful fur.

"See how much he wants it and he will not take it until I tell him," Edward continued.

"Your Grace, all should be so for you; no-one should take anything without your express consent, and all should belong to you until you choose to award it." Thomas said.

"Kill, Bragge" Edward commanded. The spaniel leapt from the crouched position onto the sticky marchpane mouse and devoured it, carpet fluff and all.

"Most excellent, Your Grace, Bragge is indeed a loyal hound." Thomas said smiling and clapping the boy on the back.

Edward wiped his sticky fingers on his knees. The broad smile had fallen from his face. "It's only Bragge who obeys me; everyone else smiles and pretends to, but I know they don't," he said, a note of petulance in his voice.

"Surely not, Your Grace, I am indeed your devoted servant. If I have ever been other you must tell me at once," Thomas said, and lowered himself to his knee before the boy with a dramatic gesture.

"Not you, Uncle. It is everyone else that treats me like a child," Edward's words were muffled as he stuffed marchpane into his mouth.

Surely not," Thomas continued, "You are your father's heir, a King in your own right."

"I wanted a purse of coins to play with Harry last week and I was told I needed to wait until my next allowance came, and to ask. *To ask!*" Edward shouted now, "I should not have to *ask*. You told me I should never have to ask anyone for anything."

"Your Grace, this is true, I am so sorry," Thomas looked truly pained by his nephew's revelation, inwardly he could not have been more pleased.

"It's not fair," bleated Edward chewing another mouthful of sweetmeats, "my father would never have allowed them to treat me like this."

"I can only humbly apologise for those who have treated your majesty so poorly." Thomas pulled from his jacket the most exquisitely embroidered purse, tasselled with gold and picked out in bright red thread, lions which sprang from the leatherwork. It was bright and gaudy, intentionally so, for it was designed to appeal to a child. "These are but the few coins I have with me and you are welcome to them all, Your Grace," Thomas let the coins spill from the purse onto the table; they were all purposefully glittering, shiny and faultless. Edward's eyes lit up.

"I shall get Harry and we can play Palermo," Edward said, reaching for the coins.

"Allow me, Your Grace," Thomas said and he smoothly scooped the coins into his hand and dropped them neatly in the purse.

Pulling the gilt strings tight, he passed the glittering parcel to his nephew.

"I have my own coffers, my own money. Why can I not have it?" Edward asked, taking the purse into his keeping.

"I do not know, Your Grace. Your Uncle…"

Edward cut him off. "He is my Uncle in name only, as Lord Protector he steps beyond the mark he should."

Thomas hid a smile. "I am sure, Your Grace that he acts only with your best interests at heart."

"His own interests are all he cares about, he keeps me from what is mine and he keeps me from my subjects and from you," Edward said sulkily.

"Surely not!" Thomas replied.

"He does. Last week before he went north to Scotland, I asked that you come to court and he told me that you were to join him on the march north and that was a lie," Edward's face was heated. "He should not lie! He cannot lie to me and yet I can do nothing when he does. You are Lord High Admiral, Master of the fleet - why would he want you to fight in the border raids with the Scots peasants?"

"I must admit I am perplexed, Your Grace," Thomas assumed a puzzled expression for Edward's benefit.

"It's to keep me here, to keep me under lock and key like the rest of my possessions.

So he knows where they are all are. I am not free to go where I will when I wish." Edward said hotly.

"Your Grace, I am so sorry, I am sure he does this only to ensure your safety," Thomas continued.

"No he doesn't, it's so he can act in my name, and I know it. I want to ride abroad, I want money, I want my lady sisters to come to see me, but they don't come even though I ask. And I cannot ride and hunt either when I wish, there is always some stupid excuse why I can't." Edward said, "If you were Lord Protector, and not your brother, would you not let me hunt when I wished, and visit where I wanted?"

Thomas could hardly hide his delight. "Indeed, Your Grace, I would of course obey your every wish, as should my brother: you are indeed our sovereign lord."

There was a pause as Edward balled more marchpane in his little fists and threw it to the vigilant spaniel.

"Who made him Lord Protector? It wasn't my father, was it? He left a council to advise me and yet he oversteps himself and now they advise him and not me," Edward said, then added, "Harry says they keep everything to themselves and think not at all to consult me. This march against Scotland, did anyone at all think to consult their King before they raised arms?"

"Your Grace, I cannot understand how this has come to be," Thomas said, "All members of your most learned Council should know you are their sovereign Lord."

"Well they don't and what can I do?" Edward's face was red, "They work against me, Uncle, and there is no-one who will help me. I have not one person I can turn to who will listen. I am a prisoner in my father's house."

Thomas dropped again to his knees in front of the young King. "Command me please my Lord, and let me show you that not all of your subjects are so faithless."

"Then I command you to get me from here and give me my rightful liberty."

"I will most humbly try. I will ask my brother Lord Protector…"

"Ask him nothing, he will not help me. You should be my lord Protector and my word should be law. Tell him."

Thomas left Edward an hour later. Promises had been made and he had what he wanted. The boy declared that he wanted him to become Lord Protector rather than his brother. If the boy declared it to be so, would that be enough. He wasn't sure. Would the council back him? Would they overrule the boy's words? They had, after all, been appointed to advise him and Thomas knew it was a council heavily-weighted in his brother's favour. The chances were they would hold fast to his brother as protector and placate the boy with hollow promises. What Edward said was true, in reality there was no-one he could complain to; until he reached majority he was very much a pawn, and at the moment he was Thomas' brother's pawn.

†

Thomas met with Harold Whitegate, a member of the Privy Council. Despite his position he remained a cautious friend of Seymour's.

"What do you think?" Thomas asked.

"The Privy Council will never accept it. They are your brother's men and he is not likely to hand over the role of Protector on the say-so of a boy. King he is, but it's in name only, and the power, Thomas, is vested in the Council; you know this."

"But if I have Edward in my possession, if he proclaims to the Council that he finds my governance more acceptable than my brother's, then surely they will have to listen?" Thomas continued to argue.

Whitegate shook his head. "You can argue with me for as long as you like, Thomas, but I will never believe the Council - and your brother - will let the King appoint you as Lord Protector. If you take him to Sudley Castle they will surely bring an army against you."

"The King's army against the King?" Thomas scoffed, "That would never happen. There are too many who are loyal to the sovereign and his wishes, and they know my power-seeking brother for what he is."

Whitegate didn't comment. Thomas probably didn't want to have himself cast in the same mould as his brother.

"Well it's set for two nights hence and I will look well on those whose support we have." Thomas concluded.

January 6th 1549

Two nights hence indeed. The key to the postern gate was in his hand. Edward's guards had already been scattered on his own orders an hour before and now he returned, as agreed with the young sovereign, to rescue him and restore him to his rightful Kingship.

Thomas Seymour entered via the postern gate. Outside, a small troop of his men waited silently with horses ready to speed their escape. The gate he left unlocked so as to hasten their passage when he returned with the young King. The corridor to the King's bedchamber was empty, there were no guards. Thomas straightened his back, smiled and walked on briskly to the bedchamber door. Edward knew he was coming and had promised to be ready. He had just to take the boys hand, retrace his steps through the King's private garden to the postern gate, then they would both be free of his brother's yoke.

Thomas did not look down as he reached for the handle to the door, and his foot made contact with Bragge keeping guard outside his master's chambers. The spaniel let out an angry howl, then began to bark incessantly.

"Bragge, be still," Thomas said. He had a knife in his hand and the dog was quiet a moment later, his throat cut. The loyal hound had served his master well and Thomas could already hear feet pounding along the marble corridor towards him.

The bed chamber door flung open and Edward, dressed as agreed, stood on the threshold and howled with anguish. Thomas, the blooded knife still in his hand and the limp pup at his feet, couldn't even think of a word to say as they reached him, grasped his hands and dragged him away from Edward.

✝

Thomas would live in the tower for a little over two months before his own brother's shaky signature at the bottom of the warrant sent him to the block. Even in the Tower, when he penned his final words, Thomas still believed he'd acted with nothing but honourable intentions.

Forgetting God to love a King
Hath been my rod

March 20th, 1549

It was cold; the wind came in from the North and bore with it a fine rain that blanketed everything with its soaking cold touch. Feet were numbed by the cold ground and hands were pushed deep into pockets to keep them warm as the gathered crowd waited on Tower Green.

There had been no trial for Thomas Seymour, an Act of Attainder listing no less than thirty-three charges against him and signed by his own brother had brought him on his final journey. Included within charges were his plans to marry Princess Elizabeth and his plot to take control of Edward and steal the boy away from his brother's control.

Richard watched from a distance. There was never any glory in an end made by the headsman's axe and he barely recognised his former master as he was led to the scaffold. The oak platform stood four feet high, the block waiting for him in its centre and a hand rail running around the parameter of the platform at waist height. Thomas Seymour was not restrained: it was expected that the nobility behave with honour at their executions and Thomas's face gave nothing away as he approached the steps to the scaffold. A cold day and they had allowed him his jacket, although the front was undone so he could shrug it off before he put his feet on the first step of the last six he would ever make. There was straw strewn on the platform and the wind whipped it cruelly in his face as his head drew level with the platform and his eyes could for the first time behold the block waiting for him.

Thomas Seymour swallowed hard, straightened his back and forced his legs to make the last four steps. He knew what waited for him, and it would not be long. The pain of waiting was at least now over. Eight paces to the block. He made them slowly, aware of the straw beneath the thin soles of his shoes, the creeping cold sticking his shirt to his skin. His eyes he kept on the block, his breathing he fought to keep level. Four paces to go and a surge of pure panic began to rise from within him. His heart, his poor heart, started to hammer in his chest and his throat closed. Two more paces. He could feel his knees were shaking now. He hoped it wasn't visible: after all, his brother might be watching. One more pace. He'd made it. Gasping in a gulp of air through his constricted throat he sank gladly to his knees; knees that, had there been any further to go, would have stopped supporting him, he was sure. Fitting his face into the cut out, he felt the wet wood supporting his neck and he began to pray.

Something was wrong! The block must have tipped over. Thomas instinctively threw his hands out to save himself as he fell forwards, landing on his face in the straw. It had been so quick even he had not realised he was dead.

He felt little as the axe fell. He had he supposed, hoped for a sense of relief. It was after all an end, a final end to the man who had twisted a savage knife into the guts of his life and left him with the crippled wreckage. Richard watched for a few more moments. The crowd shouted. The platform became sticky with the blood still pumping from the severed carotid and jugular. It had been quick. Thomas had been lucky and a single quick strike had severed his life.

✝

Elizabeth was at her house at Hatfield when she heard the news.

"Surely not?" Elizabeth said when Kate told her the news.

"Indeed, yesterday," Kate confirmed.

Elizabeth let out a long breath, and sat down heavily. "There will be no trial. How could they condemn him as a traitor without a trial?"

"Let's not worry about that. They have, and that means there'll be no more enquiries, will there?" Kate said. Elizabeth had been questioned by the Privy Council over her relationship with Seymour and had been interred in the tower whilst the enquiry went ahead when his marriage plans for Elizabeth became public knowledge after Katherine's death.

"There died a man of much wit and not much judgement," Elizabeth replied sadly.

"You can't feel sorry for him, can you?" Kate said looking askance at her. "Not after the way he treated poor Katherine."

"He was a man trapped by his own ambition, but he was still a likeable man," Elizabeth said.

That was true, Kate thought. His charm and looks had gained him a queen and a princess, and he'd lost them both.

Autumn 1550
Introduction to A Queen's Spy -
The first full length Novel in the
Series.

A
QUEEN'S
SPY

by Sam Burnell

"Richard Fitzwarren is joining the hunt."

The news passed quickly amongst those gathering for the hunt, spreading with it a palpable tension. When Robert Fitzwarren uttered his brother's name it was with scornful contempt. His servants exchanged expectant glances, they knew of the enmity between the two, although not the cause. When they spoke, it was quietly, in low voices, asking each other 'would he dare to come?' and 'would Robert kill him if he did?'

The mist still clung to the fields stealing the colour from the trees as the group of men readied themselves for the hunt. A mounted man at the top of the hill cast a watchful gaze upon them. Although a mile distant, the muffled conversations, the laughter and the barking of the dogs still reached his ears. It might have been a pleasant scene, had they not been hunting for him. Holding his own horse still, Richard Fitzwarren waited, although not for long.

The pack broke and a group of riders headed up the hill towards him. Richard glared at the man at their head. *This time, Robert...* He was ready for the confrontation and was surprised when the group of riders slowed and stopped a good distance away. Too late, he realised what their intention was. Hauling hard on the reins, the horse's serpentine neck twisted towards the trees, his heels hard in her sides pressing her to flight.

It was too late. Steel tipped, the wooden shaft loosed from the crossbow with a deadly accuracy and tore into her neck as the mare turned her proud head towards the sanctuary of the trees.

Taking only three more trembling steps, the dying horse collapsed beneath him, throwing him to the ground. Instinctively Richard loosed his feet from the stirrups as he fell, pushing away from her crushing body. The fall was awkward, the mare's last convulsive shake pitching him hard against a fallen bough. The snap was sickening as his left arm broke.

The mare's faltering final steps had brought him closer to the safety of the trees. Dizzy, breathing heavily and with his stomach threatening to betray him, Richard scrambled into the leafy refuge. Behind him the hooves of his pursuers' horses pounded up the hill.

Leaning heavily against a tree, eyes closed, he fought to stay conscious. Sweat beaded on his forehead, his body shook and stomach convulsed. Retching made the splintered bone grate. Richard realised his vision was darkening. *No, No, not now. Please God, not now.*

He wiped the back of his hand across his mouth, forcing himself to take even breaths.

He had been stupid, so damned stupid. What had possessed him to think his brother would do no more than confront him? He knew Robert better than that. Now they would run him to ground and he couldn't even give himself the satisfaction of a fighting end.

Biting back a cry he pushed the broken arm inside his jacket. *Damn Robert to Hell! Could this day get any worse?*

With the arm supported, the pain lessened. The trunk behind him was taking his weight and Richard was grateful for the support. With care, he drew his sword and was thankful to feel, for the last time, the familiar weight in his hand. The motto on the quillions beneath the hilt mocked him: *Let them hate so long as they fear.* Robert might hate him, but he doubted at this moment if he could instil fear in anyone.

Robert's men were closing in, thrashing their way through the small wood, shouting to each other as they searched for him. It wasn't going to be long before someone found him. Instinct tightened his grip on the leather hilt, whitening his knuckles.

As he waited, one of Robert's men tethered their horse at the forest's edge, near his dead mare, and began to walk towards him. Richard's eyes were fastened on his face, he knew he'd not see him where he leaned heavily against the tree.

Don't turn around... keep walking. Richard's gaze switched to the horse. *Could he make it?*

But, turn around the man did and only feet from Richard whose blade he found levelled at his chest. In a straight fight, on a good day, Richard would not have waited, but with a broken arm he didn't weigh his chances of success that highly. In fustian and old leather, Richard guessed the man was a servant, not one of his brother's companions.

"Hold! This is not our argument," Richard's voice was taut with pain as he delivered the words.

Richard's steel-grey eyes held the other's blue ones. The servant raised his hands in a gesture of supplication and took a measured step backward. About to push himself from the tree and make his unsteady way towards the horse, Richard stopped when another mount came crashing through the undergrowth. It was Harry: his cousin and his brother's lapdog and most ardent admirer.

"Jack, have you seen him?" the rider yelled at the servant. "Robert has placed a purse on his head."

Jesus, Harry! I was wrong. Today could indeed get worse.

Then the unexpected happened.

Jack stepped towards Harry, took hold of his boot with both hands, rived it from the stirrup and thrust him over the horse's back. Harry, wailing, landed on his back on the forest floor.

Richard needed no further invitation. He caught the reins Jack threw at him and hauled himself into the saddle. Turning the horse, he joined his rescuer and the pair pushed the horses into gallop down the hillside.

Printed in Dunstable, United Kingdom

63933561R00037